# Mixed-Up MAX

# Mixed-Up MAX

by Dick King-Smith

illustrated by Brian Floca

Troll

Text copyright © 1987 by Dick King-Smith.

Illustrations copyright © 1997 by Troll Communications L.L.C.

Published by Troll Communications L.L.C.

Planet Reader is a trademark of Troll Communications L.L.C.

This paperback edition published in 1997. Reprinted by permission of the author.

Printed in the United States of America.

10  9  8  7  6  5  4  3  2

# Chapter 1

"Your Auntie Betty has been squashed flat," said Pa Hedgehog to Ma.

"Oh, no!" cried Ma. "Where?"

"Just down the road. Across from the newsstand. That's a bad place to cross."

"Everywhere's a bad place to cross these days," said Ma. "The traffic's terrible. Do you realize, Pa, that's the third one this year, and all on my side of the family, too. First there was Grandfather, then my second cousin once

removed, and now poor old Auntie Betty. . . ."

They were sitting in a flower bed at their home, the garden of Number 5A of a row of semidetached houses on a suburban street. On the other side of the road was the Park, very popular with local hedgehogs on account of the good hunting it offered. As well as worms and slugs and snails, which the hedgehogs could find in their own gardens, there were special attractions in the Park. Mice lived under the Bandstand, feasting on the crumbs dropped from listeners' sandwiches; frogs dwelled in the Lily Pond, and in the Ornamental Gardens grass snakes slithered through the shrubbery. All these creatures were regarded as great delicacies by the hedgehogs, and they could

never resist the occasional night's outing in the Park. But to reach it, they had to cross the busy road.

"Poor old Auntie Betty," said Ma again. "It's a hard life, that's for sure."

"It's a hard death," said Pa sourly. "Talk about squashed flat, the poor old lady was . . ."

"Ssssshhhhh!" said Ma at the sound of approaching footsteps. "Not in front of the children," she whispered, as up trotted four small figures, exact miniatures of their parents except that their spines were still grayish rather than brown. Three of them—Peony, Pansy, and Petunia—were little sows, named by Ma, who was fond of flowers. Pa had agreed, reluctantly, to these names but had insisted

upon his own choice for the fourth, a little boar. Boys, he said, needed noble-sounding names, and the fourth youngster was therefore called Victor Maximilian St. George (Max for short).

Almost from the moment his eyes had opened, while his prickles were still soft and rubbery, Max had shown promise of being a bright boy, and by now his eyes, his ears, and his wits were all as sharp as his spines.

"What are you talking about, Ma?" he asked.

"Nothing," said Ma hastily.

"You wouldn't be talking about nothing," said Max, "or there wouldn't be any point in talking."

"Don't be fresh," Pa told him, "and mind your own business."

"Well, I suppose it is their business really, Pa, isn't it?" said Ma. "Or soon will be. They're bound to go exploring outside our garden before long, and we must warn them."

"You're right," said Pa. "Now then, you kids, you listen to me." And he proceeded to give his children a long lecture about the problem of road safety for hedgehogs.

Max listened carefully. Then he asked, "Do humans cross the road?"

"I suppose so," said Pa.

"But they don't get killed?"

"I don't think so," said Pa. "Never seen one lying in the road. Which I would have if they did."

"Well, then," said Max, "how do they get across safely?"

"You tell me, son. You tell me," said Pa.

"I will," said Max. "I will."

# Chapter 2

Max began his research the very next day. He slipped out of the garden at dusk, strolled along the path by the side wall of Number 5A, and crept under the front gate. Immediately

he found himself in a sea of activity.

It was the evening rush hour, and the home-going traffic was at its heaviest. Cars and motorcycles, buses and trucks thundered past, all terrifyingly close, it seemed to him. He crouched outside the gate, confused and dazzled by their bright lights. The street lamps, too, lit up the place like day, and Max, nocturnal by nature, made for the darkest spot he could find, in the shadow of a tall garbage

can. There he crouched, his heart hammering.

Gradually he grew a little more used to the din and the glare, and though he dared not move, he began to observe the humans, for numbers of pedestrians passed close by him. They were all walking on the narrow road on which he sat, a road raised above the level of the street itself by about the height of a hedgehog. "They're safe," said Max to himself, "because the noisy monsters aren't allowed up here."

He looked across the street and could see that at the far side of it there were other humans, also walking safely on a similar raised road. He did not, however, happen to see any cross the street.

"But they must cross somewhere," said Max. "There must be a place farther along the street."

A part of him, for he was very young, said that he would find out about that another time and that it would be nice to creep back under the gate to his family. But then another part of him determined to set off to see if he could find this human crossing place. The street was on a slight slope, and perhaps because of this Max chose to go in the downhill direction. He moved very slowly, keeping close to the outer walls of the front gardens, where there was some shadow. He froze, stock-still, whenever a human passed. No one noticed him.

Soon the houses gave way to a short row of stores, one of them that very newsstand across from which his Great-Aunt Betty had breathed her last. Here his progress was more difficult. The stores were still open, and Max had to choose his moment to make a dash across each brightly lit entrance.

*Phew! This is tiring. Perhaps I should go back home . . .* he thought, but then suddenly, not far ahead, he saw what he was seeking. There were humans crossing the street!

Sometimes singly, sometimes in twos and threes, sometimes in quite large groups, they stepped down from the narrow raised road and walked straight across the street with hardly a look to the left or right. Then they stepped up again on the far side, and off they went. Every time anyone wanted to cross, all the traffic stopped and waited respectfully until the way was clear again.

This then was the magic place! Here humans could cross in perfect safety! *If humans can, why not hedgehogs?* reasoned Max. *But how do people know the exact spot? How do the cars and trucks know when to stop?*

Cautiously, keeping close to the wall, he shuffled nearer until he found himself beside a tall pole on top of which was a glowing orange globe. Across the street, he could see, was a similar pole, and between these two poles the humans walked while the traffic waited.

Biding his time until a moment when there was no one about, Max crept forward to the edge of the raised road and peered down at the surface of the street. It was striped! It was striped, black and white, all the way from one side to the other. This was the secret!

# Chapter 3

By now it was quite late. The rush hour was over. The stores were closed. All was quiet. *I'll wait,* thought Max, *and then when a car or truck comes along, I'll cross in front of it.*

Soon he saw something coming. It was a truck. He was just halfway across when he suddenly realized that the truck hadn't slowed up at all and was almost on top of him, blinding him with its brilliant headlights, deafening him with its thunderous roar. It was not going to stop! Trucks only stopped for people—not hedgehogs!

The truck driver, who, until he was almost upon the crossing, had been quite unaware of the tiny pedestrian, did the only possible thing. With no time to brake or swerve, he steered so as to straddle the little animal.

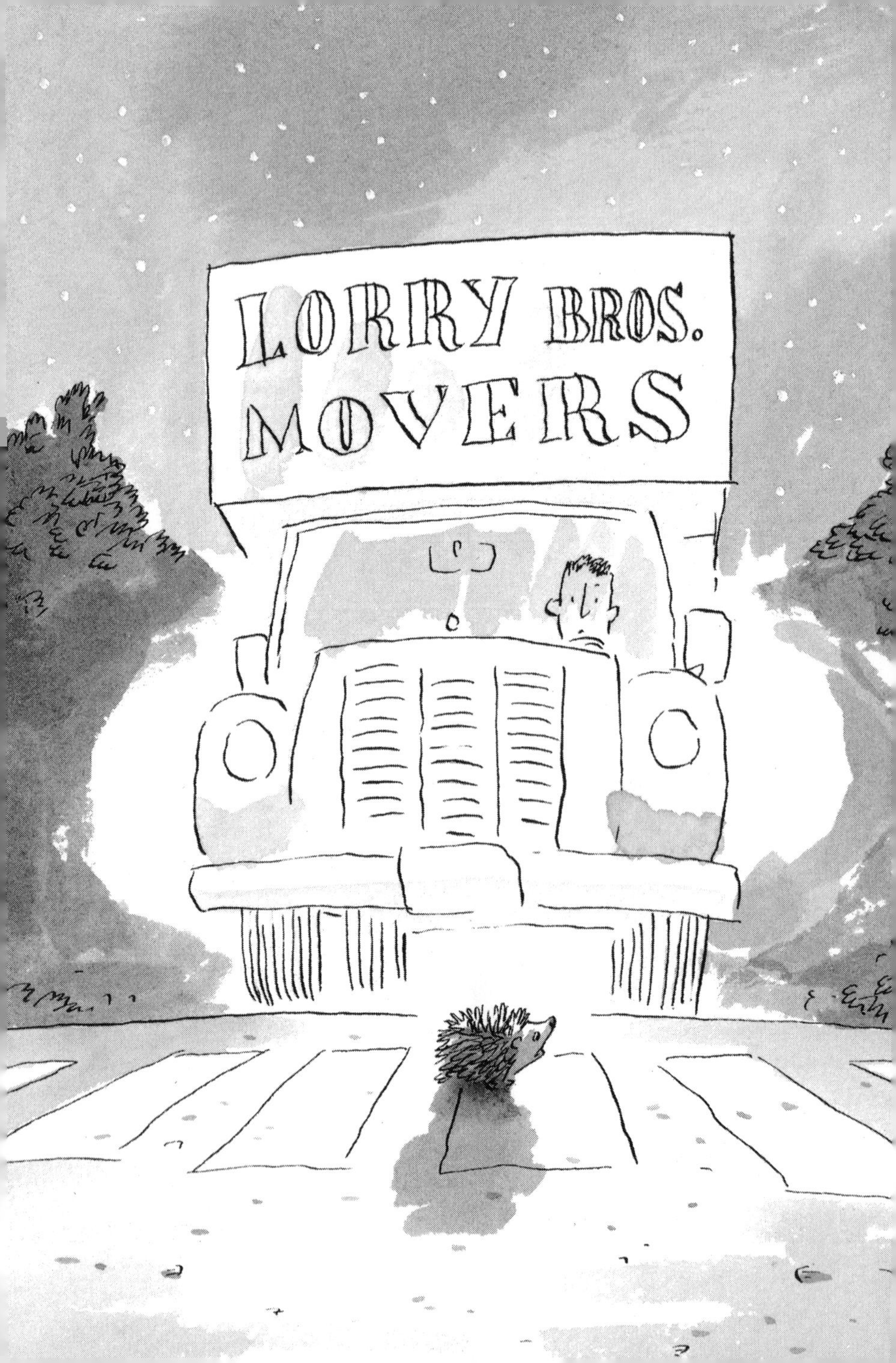
LORRY BROS.
MOVERS

Looking in his sideview mirror, he saw that it was continuing on its way unhurt, and he grinned and drove on into the night.

The sheer horror of this great monster passing above with its huge wheels on either side of him threw Max into a blind panic, and he made for the end of the crossing as fast as his legs would carry him. He did not see the bicycle rider silently pedaling along close to the curb, and the bicycle rider did not see him until the last moment. Feverishly the man twisted his handlebars, and the front wheel of the bicycle, suddenly wrenched around, caught Max on the rump and catapulted him headfirst into the curbstone.

The next thing Max recalled was crawling painfully under his own front gate. Somehow he had managed to come back over the crosswalk. He had known nothing of the concern of the bicycle rider, who had dismounted, peered at what looked like a dead hedgehog, sighed, and pedaled sadly away. Max remembered nothing of his journey home, wobbling dazedly along the now deserted sidewalk, guided only by his sense of smell. All he knew was that he had an awful headache.

The family crowded around him on his return, all talking at once.

"Where have you been all this time?" asked Ma.

"Are you all right, son?" asked Pa.

"Did you cross the road?" they both asked, and Peony, Pansy, and Petunia echoed, "Did you? Did you? Did you?"

For a while Max did not reply. His thoughts

were muddled, and when he did speak, his words were muddled, too.

"I got a head on the bump," he said slowly.

The family looked at one another.

"Something bot me on the hittom," said Max, "and then I headed my bang. My ache bads headly."

"But did you cross the road?" cried his sisters.

"Yes," said Max wearily. "I hound where the fumans cross over, but—"

"But the traffic only stops if you're a human?" interrupted Pa.

"Yes," said Max. "Not if you're a hodgeheg."

# Chapter 4

"Do you think he'll be all right?" asked Ma anxiously.

It was dawn, and they were about to retire for the day. The children were already asleep in a thick bed of fallen leaves.

"I should hope so," said Pa. "'Hodgeheg' indeed! His brains are scrambled."

Max slept around the clock and halfway around again; he did not stir until the evening of the following day. The shock had sent him into a kind of short, early hibernation.

When at last he woke, his sisters rushed to nuzzle at his nose (the safest nuzzling place for hedgehogs) with squeaks of concern. His parents left their snail hunting and came trotting up.

"How are you feeling, dear?" asked Ma.

"Yes, of course," said Max. "I'll be quite KO."

Once outside the garden gate, he turned left and headed off up the road, in the opposite direction from his previous effort. This time he was prepared for the noise and the brightness, and confident he was safe from traffic as long as he didn't step down into the road. When a human passed, he stood still. The creatures did not notice you, he found, if you did not move.

He trotted on, past the garden of Number 9A with its widow and six kids, until the row of houses ended and a factory wall began. The wall was so high that he was unable to read the sign on it beside the factory entrance: MAX SPEED 5 M.P.H., it said.

Max kept going (a good deal more slowly than this), and then suddenly, once again, he saw not far ahead what he was seeking. Again there were people crossing the street!

This time they did not go in ones and twos at random, but waited all together and then, at some signal, he supposed, crossed at the

same time. Max drew nearer, until he could hear at intervals a high, rapid beep-beep-beeping noise, at the sound of which the traffic stopped and the people walked over in safety.

Creeping closer still, tight up against the wall, he finally reached the crossing place, and now he could see this new magic method. The bunch of humans stood and watched, just above their heads, a picture of a little red man standing quite still. The people stood quite still. Then, suddenly, the little red man disappeared, and underneath the place where he had been was a picture of a little green man, walking, swinging his arms. The people walked, swinging their arms, while the high, rapid beep-beep-beeping noise warned the traffic not to move.

Max sat and watched for quite a long time, fascinated by the red man and the green man. He did wish they could have been a red hedgehog and a green hedgehog, but that was not really important, as long as hedgehogs could cross safely here. That was all he had to prove, and the sooner the better.

He edged forward, until he was just behind the waiting humans, and watched tensely for the little green man to walk.

# Chapter 5

What Max had not bargained for, when the crowd of people moved off at the beep-beep-beeping of the little green man, was that another group would be coming toward him

from the other side of the street. So that when he was about halfway across, hurrying along at the heels of one crowd, he was suddenly confronted by another. He dodged about in a forest of legs, in great danger of being stepped on. No one seemed to notice his small shape, and, indeed, he was kicked by a large foot and rolled backward.

Picking himself up, he looked across and found to his horror that the little green

man was gone and the little red man had reappeared. Frantically Max ran on as the traffic began to move. He reached the other side just inches in front of a great wheel that almost brushed his backside. The shock of so narrow an escape made him roll up, and for some time he lay in the gutter. Above his head the humans stepped onto or off the sidewalk, and the noisy green man and the silent red man lit up in turn.

After a while there seemed to be fewer people about, and Max uncurled and climbed over the curb. He turned right and set off in the direction of home. How to recross the street was something he had not yet worked out, but in his experience neither striped lines nor red and green men were the answer.

As usual he kept close to the wall at the inner edge of the sidewalk, a wall that presently gave way to iron railings. These were wide enough apart for even the largest hedgehog to pass between. Max slipped through. In the light of a full moon he could see before him a wide stretch of grass, and he ran across it until the noise and stink of the traffic were left behind.

"Am I where?" said Max, looking around him. His nose told him of the scent of flowers (in the Ornamental Gardens), his eyes told him of a strange-shaped white building (the Bandstand), and his ears told him of the sound of splashing water (as the fountain spouted endlessly in the Lily Pond).

Of course! This was the place Pa had told them all about! This was the Park!

"Hip, hip, roohay!" cried Max to the moon, and away he ran.

For the next few hours he trotted busily around the Park, shoving his snout into everything. Like most children, he was not only nosy but noisy, too, and at the sound of his coming the mice scuttled off under the Bandstand, the snakes slid away through the Ornamental Gardens, and the frogs plopped into the safe depths of the Lily Pond. Max caught nothing.

At last he began to feel rather tired and to think how nice it would be to go home to bed. But which way was home?

Max considered this and came to the unhappy conclusion that he was lost. Just then he saw, not far away, a hedgehog crossing the path, a rather large hedgehog, a Pa-sized hedgehog! What good luck! Pa had crossed the street to find him! He ran forward, but when he reached the animal, he found it was a complete stranger.

"Oh," said Max, "I peg your bardon. I thought you were a different hodgeheg."

The stranger looked curiously at him. "Are you feeling all right?" he asked.

"Yes, thank you," said Max. "The trouble is, I go to want home. But I won't know the day."

"You mean . . . you don't know the way."

"Yes."

"Well, where do you live?" asked the strange hedgehog.

"Number 5A."

"Indeed? Well, now, listen carefully, young

man. Go up this path—it will take you back to the street—and a little way along you'll see a strange sort of house that humans use. It's a tall house, just big enough for one human to stand up in, and it has windows on three sides. If you cross there, you'll end up right by your own front gate. OK?"

"KO," said Max, "and thanks."

As soon as he was through the Park's railings, he saw the tall house. He trotted up close to it. It was lit up, and sure enough, there

was a human inside it. He was holding something to his ear, and Max could see that his lips were moving. *How odd,* thought Max, getting very close now. *He's standing in there talking to himself!*

At that instant the man put down the receiver and pushed open the door of the telephone booth, a door designed to clear the sidewalk by about an inch. It was the perfect height for giving an inquisitive young hedgehog—for the second time in his short life—a tremendous bump on the head.

# Chapter 6

Meanwhile, back at Number 5A, Pa had had a bonanza. Sneaking next door and finding a full bowl of dog food and no sign of his neighbor, he had gobbled it all.

He came staggering back, very full of himself and Munchimeat, and fell into a deep, bloated sleep.

Ma woke him just before dawn. "Pa," she said. "Wake up. Max hasn't come back."

Pa opened his eyes and saw her worried face and the three smaller but equally worried faces of Peony, Pansy, and Petunia.

"He's been gone all night," said Ma. "Oh, Pa, do you think something's happened to him?"

Pa got to his feet. "I don't know," he said. "But don't worry, Ma. I'll find him."

"But he could be anywhere. How are you

going to know where to look?" Before Pa could answer, he heard a strange voice coming from the hedge that divided 5A and 5B.

"Excuse me," said the strange voice, and out poked the head of their neighbor. Pa bristled, his spines standing on end. *I'll bet it's that Munchimeat,* he thought. *He's found his empty bowl, and he's going to get tough about it. Well, I can play tough, too. I don't like the look of him anyway, and if he wants a fight he can have one. We'll soon see who's the better hog.*

But before Pa could think of anything to

say, the hedgehog from 5B came out of the hedge and said again, "Excuse me."

"Well?" said Pa.

"I couldn't help overhearing what you were saying."

"Family matter," growled Pa.

"Exactly. You're worried about your little boy."

"Oh!" cried Ma. "Have you seen him?"

"Yes, I have. At least, I met a young man in the Park who said he was lost and looking for the way back to 5A. Unless, of course, it was a 5A in some other street."

"Did you notice anything . . . different about him?" asked Ma quickly.

The neighbor looked a bit embarrassed.

"Well, yes," he said, "now that you mention it. He seemed to be having some difficulty with his speech—muddled his words now and then."

"Like 'hodgeheg'?"

"Yes."

"That's our Max!" cried Ma.

"Was he all right?" asked Pa. "Not hurt or anything?"

"No, he was fine. I told him the best way to go home. He'll be back soon, I'm sure. Try not to worry."

Pa cleared his throat awkwardly. His neighbor's kindness added greatly to his feelings of guilt.

"It's very thoughtful of you," he said.

"Glad to help. That's what neighbors are for."

"Can we offer you something?" asked Ma. "Some bread and milk?"

"Oh, no, thanks," said the neighbor. "I had

a pretty good night's hunting in the Park. Just as well, because when I got home I found that something had eaten all my Munchimeat." He looked directly at Pa, and his eyes were twinkling. "It was a cat, I suppose," he said, and back through the hedge he went.

"Wasn't that nice of him!" said Ma.

Peony, Pansy, and Petunia chanted, "Nice! Nice! Nice!"

Pa grunted. A part of him thought he should confess his sin to his neighbor. But then another part of him, for he was very worldly-wise, thought the less said the better. Life was full enough of headaches without inviting any extra ones.

The same thought occurred to Max when at last he came to his senses. The door of the telephone booth had knocked him out cold. The neighbor from 5B had not noticed the still, small figure as he hurried to cross the deserted street before the morning rush hour began.

*Oh,* thought Max, *has any hedgehog ever*

*had a more horrible headache? The last bump I got made me talk funny, and I bet this one's made things even worse. I'd better try saying something.*

"Oh," said Max, "has any hedgehog ever had a more horrible headache?" Max considered this. It sounded fine. Suddenly he felt fine. Even the ache already felt much less.

"My name," he said quietly, "is Victor Maximilian St. George, and," he said more loudly, "I have three sisters named Peony, Pansy, and Petunia, and I live with Pa and Ma at Number 5A, and," he shouted at the top of his voice, "I am a very lucky HEDGEHOG!" And without thinking, without listening, without a single glance to the left or to the right, he dashed across the street, right in front of the first of the morning's vehicles—the milk truck.

The noise that followed was enough to wake the whole street.

First there was a screech as the milkman braked and swerved, and then came the

shattering sound of dozens and dozens of bottles smashing. Last came the sound of the milkman's voice cursing every hedgehog ever born as he danced with rage in a sea of Gold Top and Silver Top, of two-percent and skimmed, of orange juice and grapefruit juice and fresh farm eggs.

Ma and Pa had sent the girls to bed and were waiting up in the growing light of dawn. They were crouching side by side listening, when suddenly the dreadful noise burst upon their ears.

"Sounds like something's got run over," said Pa heavily. "Brace yourself, old lady. It could be our Max."

Ma buried her head and rolled herself into a ball of misery.

At that moment they heard Max's cheery voice.

"Now, now!" he said. "What's all the fuss about? There's no point in crying over spilled milk!"

# Chapter 7

What a happy scene of grunting, snuffling, squeaking joy there was in the garden of 5A as the girls were woken to be told the good news! And what a jolly crunching of snails there was as the family celebrated with a feast! After it all, Max went to bed and slept heavily. By evening, when he reappeared, the neighbor had come through the hedge twice, once to inquire if Max was back and again to ask if he was quite well after his adventure.

At first Ma and Pa felt more than a little uncomfortable at these visits, Ma because she knew what Pa had done, Pa because he knew that the neighbor knew. But the matter was not mentioned.

They had been wrong, they found, in supposing that a family of hedgehogs lived next door. The neighbor had never married, and as elderly bachelors often are, he was rather lonely and very fond of children. Already he had invited Peony, Pansy, and Petunia to come and play in his garden whenever they liked, and seeing that they were not sure how to address him, he had asked them to call him "Uncle."

"Uncle what?" they asked.

The kindly neighbor scratched his head thoughtfully with his hind foot.

"Let's see now," he said. "I live in the garden of Number 5B. How about 'Uncle B.'?"

After dark the family was worm hunting on the lawn when there was a rustling in the dividing hedge. The three girls ran toward it, crying, "Uncle B.! Uncle B.! Uncle B.!"

"Who's Uncle B.?" asked Max.

"Our next-door neighbor," said Ma. "That's what the girls call him. They've been playing in his garden."

"But, Pa," said Max, "I thought you couldn't stand him?"

Pa was saved from replying by the approach of Uncle B., and now Max recognized him.

"Oh, hello, sir," he said politely. "You're the gentlehog I met in the Park. Thank you very much for your help."

"Don't mention it, Max," said Uncle B. "I'm glad to hear from your parents that you're, uhhh . . . totally recovered."

"You should stay in the garden, son," said Pa. "You're safe in here."

Max considered this. He had no intention of giving up his research. The neighbor had helped him once. Maybe he could do so again. As if reading his thoughts Uncle B. said, "Well,

I must be running along now. Any time you feel like having a chat, Max, you just come on over."

The next night Max stopped by.

"Hello, young fellow," said Uncle B. "Have some Munchimeat. They always give me more than I can eat."

"No, thanks. It's your advice I need," said Max, getting straight to the point.

"Shoot," said Uncle B.

He listened carefully while Max told him everything that had happened so far in his efforts to find a safe hedgehog crossing. "I must say," he said when Max had finished, "I admire your spirit. And your ambition. Finding a really safe way to cross roads would benefit the whole of hedgehogkind. But the two methods that humans use don't seem to be suitable for us. No better, it appears from your experiences, than the old time-honored way—look right, look left, look right again, before going across. One thing strikes me, however . . . " Uncle B. paused.

"What's that, Uncle B.?"

"All your research so far has been at nighttime because hedgehogs are nocturnal. But humans aren't. They don't see at all well at night, which is why they keep running us over. Now, if you could only find a place to cross in broad daylight, then at least they could see us coming. It might pay us to change our habits. Better to lose your sleep than your life, that's what I say."

"Well," said Max, "I suppose either of the two ways I've tried would work in daylight, too. The trouble is, with either of them, you've got to get across so quickly. If only there were a human who could stop traffic and make absolutely sure it didn't move until you were safely across."

"There are humans like that," said Uncle B. "I saw one once, when I was out during the day—not something I often do. He was a big man dressed in blue, with a hat on his head. He just held up his hand, and everything stopped while some small humans crossed the street. Once they were safely on the other side, he waved the traffic on again."

Max pondered this. "So," he said, "there might be lots and lots of small humans who have to cross the street by day?"

Uncle B. nodded.

"And the big humans," Max continued, "would worry about the small ones getting across safely?"

"Oh, yes. Just like hedgehogs."

"So there must be a special, perfectly safe daytime crossing place for small humans— now where could that be?"

"You tell me, Max. You tell me," said Uncle B.

"I will," said Max. "I will!"

# Chapter 8

Max could hardly wait for the next dawn. Something inside him said that today he would at last be successful in his quest, and outside him every one of his five thousand spines tingled with excitement. The more he thought of his conversation with Uncle B., the more he felt convinced that the answer to the problem lay with the small humans. Their crossing place must be the safest. Follow them and he would find it.

He waited until the family was fast asleep, and then, blinking in the unaccustomed sunlight, he went along the path by the side wall of Number 5A to the front gate. He did not go under it but waited, watching beneath it. Already he had learned that you could tell the age of humans from the size of their feet, and he

settled himself to wait patiently until a pair of
small ones came past. When at last they did, he
was about to go out and follow, but then another
pair went by and then several pairs. As the
sidewalk filled up with school-going children,

dozens and dozens of small feet went walking, dancing, skipping, hopping past his gate.

All of them were going in the same direction, to his left, up the road, which would take them, he knew, to the end of the row of houses and past the factory to the red man and the green man. Was that, after all, where all small humans crossed? He must follow, he must know for sure.

At last, when it seemed to him that no more feet were coming, Max crept under his gate and set out. Some way ahead he could see the tail of the procession, and he hurried after it. He had passed the last of the houses and reached the factory entrance when he saw that the children were taking no notice of the changing red and green men. They were going to a spot farther on. And they were crossing over the road there!

He ran on (under the sign MAX SPEED 5 M.P.H.—and he wasn't far short of it) until he was close enough to see exactly what was going on. And oh, what a scene it was!

"Oh, what a scene it was!" he told the family and Uncle B. that evening. "There was this great big human—it was a female, I could tell by the voice. She was dressed in a long white coat, and she had a black cap with a peak. She carried a tall pole, and on top of the pole was a big round white disk with an orange rim and

CAUTION. CHILDREN CROSSING

black marks on it—a magic wand it must have been, because she walked out into the middle of the street and held it up, and all the traffic stopped dead!"

He paused for breath.

"Then what?" asked Pa.

"Then all the small humans went across, and the great big female just stood there until the very last one reached the other side safely. And all that time everything stood absolutely still. Buses, trucks, cars, motorcycles, not one of them dared move an inch for fear of the great female and her magic wand!"

"Where did the small humans go, Max?" asked Uncle B.

"Into a huge building," said Max. "And I hid myself and watched all day. At the end of the afternoon they all came out of the building again, and there was the great female waiting for them, in her white coat and her black hat. She waved her wand again and saw them safely back across. I tell you, it's the ideal place for us—the huge building's right next to the Park. Nothing would ever dare touch us if we were under the protection of that powerful human!"

"But I don't want to spend the daytime in the Park," said Pa. "Setting out in the morning and coming back in the afternoon—that's no good for me. I need a good day's sleep."

"You could still get that, old hog," said Uncle B. "You could go over in the morning, find a nice place to lie down—under the Bandstand, let's say—get your eight hours, have a good night's hunting, and come back the following morning. Do it once a week, perhaps. You could take your wife and the girls. It'd make a nice outing."

"Oh, please, Pa! Please! Please!" cried Peony, Pansy, and Petunia.

Pa considered this. "One of us ought to try it first. See if it works," he said. "And if anyone's going, it's me."

"Not without me," said Ma bravely.

"Why not let me go," said Uncle B. "After all, I've had a good long life. If anything goes wrong, there'll be no one to miss me."

"Oh, yes, there will!" cried all the family.

"Look," said Max. "You don't know which way to go, how to get there, where exactly it is. None of you can go without me."

"Well, then," said Ma, "why don't we all go?"

# Chapter 9

Very early the following morning, seven spiny shapes emerged from under the front gates of Numbers 5A and 5B. They set off up the road, passing garden after garden from many of which (like 9A) a hedgehog had set out on a journey to the Park, never to return. If only they could succeed today! Henceforth the street would be forever safe for all hedgehogkind!

They passed the factory, and the automatic

crossing with its little red and green men, and came at last to the spot where Max had seen the great female with the magic wand. Opposite them, across the street, the school clock showed six o'clock. The hedgehogs concealed themselves in a doorway and settled down to wait.

At a quarter past eight, the crossing guard arrived. Even the most punctual children never appeared before eight-thirty, but she liked to get to work ahead of time. She stood stamping her large feet, for it was a cold morning. She smoothed down her long white coat. She settled her black cap firmly. Then, grasping her staff of office, its circular disk bearing the words CAUTION. CHILDREN CROSSING,

she stood at attention at the curbside, ready for the first comers, while the rush-hour traffic roared past.

Never, for the rest of her life, would the crossing guard forget the sight that now met her eyes. Coming along the sidewalk toward

her were seven hedgehogs in single file.

"Surely you're not going to school?" asked the crossing guard when they reached her.

The noise she made meant nothing to Max, but he advanced to the edge of the curb, his nose pointing eagerly across the street, the others lined up behind him.

"We wish to go to the Park," he said. "Kindly stop the traffic."

The noise he made meant nothing to the crossing guard, but his intention was as clear as the day. Raising her magic wand high, the great female strode into the middle of the street, and at the sight of her the traffic meekly halted.

Then, before the astonished eyes of those fortunate enough to witness this historic occasion, there walked across the street a slow, solemn, dignified procession—of hedgehogs.

At the rear was Uncle B., shepherding before him Peony, Pansy, and Petunia. In front of them was Ma. In front of her was Pa. But at the head of the line there marched that pioneer of road safety Victor Maximilian St. George, a name to be remembered forever by hedgehogs the world over.

"Tell us the story of the First Crossing, Mommy," little hedgehogs would plead at bedtime, and then they would listen, enthralled, to the tale of Max, the hedgehog who became a hodgeheg who became a hero. And always the mothers ended with the same words:

"... and they all crossed happily ever after!"

## About the Author

**Dick King-Smith** has been a farmer and a teacher as well as an award-winning author of children's books. His book *Babe: The Gallant Pig* was adapted into the hugely successful movie *Babe*.

Mr. King-Smith lives in Gloucestershire, England, the place where he was born.

## About the Illustrator

**Brian Floca** is the author and illustrator of *The Frightful Story of Harry Walfish,* and he is the illustrator of *Jenius: The Amazing Guinea Pig* by Dick King-Smith. Mr. Floca also illustrated *Poppy* by Avi (winner of the 1996 *Boston Globe-Horn Book* Award for fiction) and *Luck with Potatoes* (a *Boston Globe* "Best of '95" children's book).

Mr. Floca lives and works in Somerville, Massachusetts.